RAINBOW
magic
The Ocean Fairies

...Rosemary Scarborough, a very
special friend of the fairies!

Special thanks
to Narinder Dhami

ORCHARD BOOKS
338 Euston Road, London NW1 3BH
Orchard Books Australia
Level 17/207 Kent Street, Sydney, NSW 2000
A Paperback Original

First published in 2010 by Orchard Books

HiT entertainment

A CIP catalogue record for this book is available
from the British Library.

ISBN 978 1 40830 818 9

JS

1 3 5 7 9 10 8 6 4 2

Printed in Great Britain

The paper and board used in this paperback are natural recyclable
products made from wood grown in sustainable forests. The
manufacturing processes conform to the environmental regulations
of the country of origin.

Orchard Books is a division of Hachette Children's Books,
an Hachette UK company.

www.hachette.co.uk

Tess
the Sea Turtle
Fairy

by Daisy Meadows

ORCHARD BOOKS

www.rainbowmagic.co.uk

The Fairyland Palace

GALA
FAIRYLAND ROYAL AQUARIUM

Fairyland Royal Aquarium

Kirsty's Gran's House

Lighthouse

The Park

Rockpool

Lea-On-Sea

Ocean Star Sailing Ship

Whales

The Magical Conch Shell at my side,
I'll rule the oceans far and wide!
But my foolish goblins have shattered the shell,
So now I cast my icy spell.

Seven shell fragments, be gone, I say,
To the human world to hide away,
Now the shell is gone, it's plain to see,
The oceans will never have harmony!

Contents

A Magical Sandcastle

"Shall we build another tower, Kirsty?" Rachel Walker asked her best friend, Kirsty Tate.

The two girls were kneeling on the beach, making an enormous sandcastle. They'd been working on it all day in the sunshine. The castle had turrets and towers and archways.

"Oh, yes, brilliant idea!" Kirsty said with a grin. She picked up her bucket. "Let's start decorating the castle, too. We can use those pretty pink and white shells we found earlier."

Carefully, Rachel began to build the tower. Meanwhile Kirsty tipped the shells out of her bucket and began sorting through them.

"Look, Kirsty, the sun's starting to set," Rachel pointed out, noticing that people were packing up and leaving the beach.

"We'll have to go back to your gran's soon." The girls were spending the spring school holiday in Leamouth with Kirsty's gran.

Kirsty's face fell. "I know we've had a lovely time on the beach, Rachel," she sighed, "but we haven't seen a *single* magical fairy sparkle all day! I was hoping we were going to find another missing piece of the Magical Golden Conch Shell."

"Me, too," Rachel agreed. "But don't forget what Queen Titania always says – we *have* to wait for the magic to come to us!"

On the first day of their holiday, the girls had been thrilled to receive an invitation to the Fairyland Ocean Gala. There they'd met their old friend, Shannon the Ocean Fairy, as well as the other Ocean Fairies and their Magical Creatures. The highlight of the gala was to be the moment when Shannon played the beautiful Golden Conch Shell. This would make sure that there was peace, harmony and order in all the oceans of the world for the next year.

But before Shannon had a chance to play her magical tune, Jack Frost and his goblins had burst onto the scene. On Jack Frost's orders, the goblins had grabbed the Golden Conch Shell, but as they argued over it, the Conch Shell had fallen to the ground and smashed into seven shining pieces.

Jack Frost had immediately raised his ice wand and, with a burst of freezing magic, he'd scattered the seven fragments in different hiding places throughout the human world. Shannon, Rachel, Kirsty, and all the fairies had been horrified.

They knew that without the Golden Conch Shell, there would be chaos and confusion in the oceans.

"It doesn't look like any magic is going to come to us today, though," Kirsty remarked. She began pressing rows of tiny, creamy shells onto the sides of the sandcastle. "But at least we've helped the Ocean Fairies find three pieces of the Golden Conch Shell so far."

"And we know that four of the Magical Ocean Creatures are still guarding the four missing pieces," Rachel pointed out.

Luckily, Queen Titania had acted quickly to limit the power of Jack Frost's spell. The queen had used her own magic to send the Ocean Fairies' Magical Creatures out into the human world to guard the shell fragments until they were found and returned safely to Fairyland. Then the Golden Conch Shell could magically repair itself and Shannon would be able to play it at last.

"Isn't our castle great, Rachel?" Kirsty said proudly, sitting back on her heels to take a look. There was hardly anyone left on the beach now besides the two girls.

Rachel nodded. "It looks a bit like the Fairyland Palace with all those towers," she replied. "Except our castle isn't so sparkly, of course!"

Suddenly Kirsty gave an excited cry.

"Are you *sure*, Rachel?" she asked with a big smile. "Look in there, under that archway!"

Rachel bent forward on her hands and knees and peered inside the sandcastle. Then she saw it! A glittering, golden light was shining right in the very centre of the castle.

"Kirsty, I think it's a fairy!" Rachel gasped, spotting a tiny figure dancing gracefully through the sandy rooms. "It's Tess the Sea Turtle Fairy!"

Tess fluttered over to the archway and waved up at the girls. She wore cropped blue trousers and a pale blue sparkly T-shirt with an aquamarine cardi over the top. Her silky blonde hair was braided in two bouncy plaits.

"Girls, I'm so glad to see you," Tess called in a silvery voice. "Come and join me inside your beautiful sandcastle!" She pointed her wand at Rachel and Kirsty

and a stream of sparkles swirled around
them. The girls felt themselves shrinking
as they'd done so many times before, and
in the twinkle of an eye, they were fairy-
sized with gossamer wings just like Tess's.

Quickly, Rachel and Kirsty flew under
the archway and joined their fairy friend
inside the sandcastle.

"We're really pleased to see you, Tess!" Kirsty beamed at the fairy. "Have you found another piece of the Golden Conch Shell?"

Tess nodded. "I think so," she replied. "My magical sea turtle friend, Pearl, is guarding it. But it's far away from here in a tropical land. Will you come with me, girls?"

"Of course we will!" cried Rachel eagerly.

"Gran isn't expecting us home just yet," Kirsty added. "Let's go right away!"

Turtle Trouble

Waving her wand, Tess flew around
Rachel and Kirsty as they hovered in
the air.

Immediately a dazzling cloud of fairy
sparkles surrounded the girls. They closed
their eyes and felt themselves whisked
away from Leamouth beach, whizzing
through the air at a speed that took their
breath away.

Suddenly the air felt much warmer. Rachel and Kirsty opened their eyes and saw that they were flying over a tropical beach. The ocean was a clear aquamarine colour, and the sand was a pure, soft white. Palm trees fringed the shore, their leafy fronds waving in the gentle breeze. It was dusk, like it had been in Leamouth, and the pink and gold sun was sinking slowly into the rippling water.

"Oh, isn't it beautiful?" Kirsty sighed happily. She peered down at the beach as it began to get a little darker. "I wish we'd got here a bit earlier so that we could see it all in the daylight."

Rachel was squinting down at the beach, too. "What are *those?*" she asked, sounding puzzled. "They look like little polka dots, but they're running around – and there are *lots* of them!"

At first Kirsty couldn't see what Rachel meant, but as her eyes adjusted to the dim light, she too could see little round shapes. They were scurrying across the sand in every direction.

"Let's fly a bit closer," said Tess, "and then you'll be able to see what they are!"

Curious, Rachel and Kirsty followed Tess as she floated down towards the beach.

"Oh!" Kirsty exclaimed suddenly. "They're baby sea turtles!"

"Aren't they cute?" Rachel laughed.

The little green turtles were using their tiny flippers to move across the beach away from the ocean. As the girls watched, they saw sand flying in all directions and more baby turtles began to appear from holes in the ground.

"Those are the ones that have just hatched," Tess explained. "The mother turtle buries her eggs under the sand."

"But why are all the baby turtles running away from the ocean?" Kirsty asked.

Tess sighed. "When baby sea turtles hatch, they *should* head straight for the water," she explained. "But the poor little things are confused, like the other ocean creatures, because all the pieces of the Golden Conch Shell haven't been found yet!"

Kirsty and Rachel shared an anxious glance. "What will happen to them?" Kirsty asked.

"Can we help?"

"Maybe we can carry them to the ocean and put them in the water," Rachel suggested.

"No, there are far too many!" Tess replied, glancing down at the hundreds of tiny turtles below them. "We must find Pearl. Then she'll be able to lead the babies safely to the ocean."

"Shall we fly around and look for her?" asked Rachel.

Tess nodded. "But stay close to the beach," she told them.

Rachel and Tess flew off in different directions along the beach. Meanwhile, Kirsty zoomed over to the palm trees and began to zigzag slowly between them, keeping a sharp look out for Pearl.

Suddenly a loud voice coming from the treetops overhead almost made Kirsty jump out of her skin.

"My feet are cold and wet! I HATE having cold, wet feet!"

Kirsty froze in mid air and glanced upwards, but she couldn't see anything. Quickly she whizzed back to the beach.

"Rachel! Tess!" Kirsty called to her friends. "Over here!"

"Have you found Pearl?" Rachel asked eagerly as she and Tess rushed to join Kirsty.

"No, but come and listen to this!"

Kirsty told them. She led Rachel and Tess
over to the palm trees. As they hovered
there, they heard a shrill, complaining
voice above them.

"My feet are cold and wet, too! There's
horrid, itchy sand between my toes!"

Kirsty glanced at Rachel and Tess. "Did
you hear that?" she whispered. "Goblins!"

Follow the Leader

Tess frowned. "It *sounds* like goblins,"
she replied. "We all know they don't like
having cold, wet feet! Let's take a look."

Tess flew upwards, towards the voice,
and Rachel and Kirsty followed. Suddenly
they heard the sound of Tess's tinkling
fairy laughter.

"Girls, these are the most handsome
goblins I've ever seen!" she called.

Surprised, Rachel and Kirsty flew higher. Then their eyes widened and they too burst out laughing. Four beautiful scarlet and blue parrots were perched on the top of the palm tree. As Tess and the girls watched, one of the parrots opened his beak and squawked, "I hate sand!"

"I hate sand!" the parrot sitting beside him repeated crossly.

"The parrots are mimicking the sound of the goblins grumbling and arguing!" Rachel said with a grin.

"But that means there *must* be goblins around here *somewhere*," Kirsty pointed out.

Tess nodded. "So it's even more important that we find the missing piece of the Golden Conch Shell before the goblins do," she said anxiously. "I wonder where Pearl is? She's the only one who can help us."

"Let's carry on searching," said Rachel.

Tess and the girls flew off along the beach again, above the baby turtles who were still scurrying around. It was almost dark now, but there was a large pale moon, and stars were beginning to sparkle in the midnight-blue sky.

"Doesn't the moonlight make everything look magical?" Kirsty remarked, staring out over the waves gently lapping the shore. Then she blinked, wondering if she was seeing things. Was that a golden glow out there on the water, glittering in the light of the moon?

"There's something shiny and sparkly in the ocean!" Kirsty shouted excitedly. "I think it might be a missing piece of the Conch Shell!"

Rachel and Tess gazed in the direction Kirsty was pointing.

"It looks like the waves are carrying it to the shore," Rachel said, her eyes fixed on the sparkling glow.

"Come on, girls!" Tess cried, zooming off towards the water.

Rachel and Kirsty rushed after her and the three friends hovered in the air as the glowing object floated closer to the beach.

"It's not a missing piece of the Conch Shell," Tess exclaimed with delight. "It's Pearl!"

Rachel and Kirsty watched the magical green sea turtle swim gracefully through the waves and onto the shore. Pearl's beautiful shell glittered with fairy magic as she pulled herself higher up the sand with her strong flippers.

"I'm so glad you found us, Pearl!" Tess flew down and stroked the turtle's head. "We need your help."

"Yes, the baby turtles are running *away*

from the ocean, instead of towards it," Rachel explained. "And we know there are goblins around here somewhere because the parrots are talking like them!" Kirsty added.

Slowly Pearl nodded her head, her dark eyes wise and kind. "The missing piece of the Golden Conch Shell is around here somewhere, but I'm not quite sure where," she explained. "I saw it bobbing around on the waves, but then I lost sight of it. I think it might have been washed up on the shore."

"Maybe we should look after the baby turtles first, and lead them safely to the water," Tess suggested. "I'm very worried about them. Then we can start searching for the shell."

Rachel glanced down at the beach below them. To her surprise, she saw that the baby turtles had stopped running aimlessly away from the ocean. Instead they were all scuttling along the beach, heading the same way in one big crowd.

"What's going on?" Rachel wondered. Then, at the front of the crowd of turtles, she spotted a group of three children wandering along the beach. One of them was carrying a bucket. "Look," Rachel went on, surprised, "I think the baby turtles are following those children!"

"Let's find out," Tess said. She
flew off with Rachel and Kirsty right
behind her, and Pearl followed them
along the sand.

As Tess and the girls got closer to the
children, they noticed something very odd.

"Why are they wearing big straw
hats and sunglasses?" Kirsty whispered,
frowning. "The sun's gone down, and
it's dark!"

"Look at their footprints, too." Tess
pointed down at the sand. "They have
very big feet for children."

"And very big ears!" Rachel said in
a low voice, spotting large, pointy ears
sticking out of the straw hats. "They're
not children at all. They're goblins!"

Tess, Kirsty and Rachel glanced at
each other in dismay.

"But why are the baby turtles following them?" Kirsty asked, confused, glancing down at the large crowd of turtles still scurrying along behind the goblins.

Tess grinned. "Well, the turtles have only just hatched," she replied. "And since they're green, and so are the goblins, the babies think the goblins are grown-up turtles!"

Pogwurzle Panic

Rachel and Kirsty couldn't help laughing.

"I wonder if the goblins know they're being followed?" said Rachel.

"And *I* wonder what the goblins have got in that bucket!" Kirsty whispered.

Suddenly the biggest goblin happened to glance around and see the baby turtles. He gave a shriek of fear and peered nervously down at the tiny creatures.

"Look!" the goblin yelled, squinting through the darkness. "We're being followed by – I don't know *what* they are!"

The other two goblins spun round.

"What are you so scared of?" the goblin with the bucket asked scornfully. "They're only little, whatever they are. They can't hurt us!"

"They can if they're baby *pogwurzles!*" the third goblin gasped.

All three goblins yelped with fright this time.

"Ooh, pogwurzles!" groaned the goblin with the bucket, backing away from the baby turtles. "I hate pogwurzles even more than I hate sand between my toes!"

"Shoo!" shouted the biggest goblin. He whipped his straw hat off and began flapping it at the baby turtles. The others did the same. "Go back to Pogwurzle Land!"

The baby turtles took no notice.

"They're going to attack us!" the goblin with the bucket shouted as the turtles came closer. "Run for your life!" And all three goblins raced off along the beach in a panic, leaving the turtles behind them.

"After them!" Tess cried.

Tess and the girls dashed after the goblins while Pearl followed behind, keeping an eye on the baby turtles.

When the goblins spotted Tess, Rachel
and Kirsty flying overhead, they scowled
and ran even faster.

"Pesky fairies *and* scary pogwurzles!" the
biggest goblin groaned. "Go away!"

Kirsty noticed that the goblin holding the bucket was looking very worried. He was gripping the bucket tightly with both hands, keeping it very close to him.

"What's in your bucket?" Kirsty called as she, Tess and Rachel flew alongside the goblins.

"None of your business!" the goblin yelled. "I'm *not* telling you what we found—"

The biggest goblin skidded to a halt and immediately clapped his hand over the first goblin's mouth.

"Keep your big goblin mouth shut!" he ordered angrily. "Those fairies are just trying to trick us into telling them that—"

Quickly the third goblin clapped *his* hand over the biggest goblin's mouth.

"Don't tell our secret, blabbermouth!" he shouted.

Furiously the biggest goblin slapped his hand away.

"Now the fairies and the pogwurzles *know* that we have a secret!" he snapped.

"You've given the game away!"

"No, I haven't!" the third goblin retorted. "They don't know that we found the—"

"Shut up!" the first and second goblins shrieked frantically. "Don't say anything!"

"I think there's a missing piece of the Golden Conch Shell in that bucket," Kirsty whispered to Rachel and Tess. "I'm going to take a look!"

As the goblins argued fiercely about
what they should or shouldn't say, Kirsty
flew towards the goblin with the bucket.
But just as she was about to peep inside it,
the goblin spotted her.

"Leave me alone!" he shouted, whisking
the bucket away from Kirsty.

"Let's help Kirsty by distracting the
goblins," Tess murmured to Rachel, and
they flew to join her.

"Be careful," Rachel called. "The baby pogwurzles are catching up with you!"

All three goblins moaned with terror as Tess and Rachel fluttered around them.

"The pogwurzles are going to nibble our toes!" the goblin with the bucket gasped.

As he turned to glance at the baby turtles, who were getting closer again, Kirsty saw her chance. She flew down once more and this time she managed to get a glimpse inside the bucket.

Sure enough, there lay a piece of the missing Golden Conch Shell, glinting in the moonlight!

Pearl and a Plan

Excited, Kirsty waved at Rachel and Tess.

"It's here!" she mouthed silently, pointing at the bucket.

The goblins hadn't noticed Kirsty this time. They were huddled together, staring in panic at the baby turtles, who'd also come to a stop as they waited for the goblins to start moving again.

"We can't get away from these baby pogwurzles," the biggest goblin muttered. "They're going to follow us all the way back to Jack Frost's Ice Castle!"

"And then Jack Frost will be *really* angry with us," the third goblin added. "We need a plan to get away from them. Any ideas?"

"We could jump in the sea and swim away," the goblin with the bucket suggested.

"That's a great idea," said the biggest goblin eagerly.

"Except we can't swim, you idiots!" the third goblin snapped.

As the goblins argued, Kirsty flew quickly over to Rachel and Tess.

"We need a plan, too!" Kirsty whispered. "How are we going to get the shell piece out of the bucket?"

"And how can we stop the baby turtles from following the goblins, and lead them back to the ocean?" Rachel added.

Tess's face lit up. "Pearl can help us do *both*!" she replied with a beaming smile. "Come on, girls!"

The three friends left the goblins arguing
and flew along the beach a little way to
where Pearl was waiting patiently. Tess
dipped down and whispered something to
her. "Of course," Pearl agreed, nodding
her head.

Rachel and Kirsty watched as Pearl
began to move towards the baby
turtles, pulling herself along the
sand with her flippers. As Pearl got
closer, her shell began to glow with
dazzling fairy magic, as bright as
the moon shining above them.

Slowly the baby turtles turned their heads to look at the glowing light of Pearl's shell. Then, losing interest in the goblins, they all turned and hurried towards Pearl instead.

"Look!" shouted the biggest goblin with relief. "The baby pogwurzles are going away!"

"Yippee!" yelled the other goblins, and they jumped up and down with glee.

"Let's go home to Jack Frost right away," the goblin with the bucket suggested. "He's going to be *very* pleased when he sees what we've found!"

The biggest goblin nodded. "Give me the bucket then," he said. "It's *my* turn to carry it."

"No, it isn't!" The goblin with the bucket hugged it protectively against him. "You can't have it!"

"Stop arguing, you two," said the third goblin. "*I'll* carry the bucket!"

The goblins were so busy fighting over
the bucket, they didn't notice that Pearl
was now leading the crowd of baby turtles
towards them. Rachel, Kirsty and Tess
watched as the baby turtles
followed Pearl closer to
the goblins. In just
a few moments,
the goblins were
surrounded as
the little turtles
scampered
around them.
Suddenly,
the biggest
goblin looked
down and
gave a yelp
of fear.

"The pogwurzles have sneaked up on us!" he shouted. "We're trapped!"

"Help!" shouted the goblin with the bucket, letting go of the handle in panic.

As the bucket hit the sand, the glittering piece of the Golden Conch Shell fell out and rolled towards Tess and the girls. Instantly Rachel swooped down and picked it up.

"Those fairies have our shell!" the biggest goblin yelled furiously. "We *must* get it back!"

"We can't," groaned the goblin who'd dropped the bucket. "We're surrounded by baby pogwurzles!"

"Just a minute…" The third goblin frowned as he peered more closely at the baby turtles around them. The glow from Pearl's shell was lighting up the darkness, making the turtles more visible. "I don't think these *are* baby pogwurzles," the goblin announced at last. "They don't look scary at all. It's just another fairy trick!"

The goblins scowled at Rachel, Kirsty and Tess.

"Give our shell piece back!" the biggest goblin demanded.

Tess turned to Rachel and Kirsty.

"We have to take the shell back to Fairyland before the goblins can grab it," Tess said urgently. "But first we need to guide the baby turtles safely to the ocean!"

Four Found, Three to Go!

Tess beckoned to Pearl, who nodded. The turtle hurried towards the ocean, her shell still glowing brightly, and the baby turtles began to follow.

Meanwhile Tess waved her wand around herself, Rachel and Kirsty as they hovered in the air. Suddenly a shimmering, silvery light surrounded them.

"Now the baby turtles will follow us, as well as Pearl," Tess told the girls.

Bathed in the shining glow, Tess, Rachel and Kirsty flew towards the ocean.

"The turtles are coming!" Kirsty called with delight as she looked down and saw all the babies rushing towards the water.

"STOP!" the biggest goblin roared, chasing after Tess and the girls. "Give us the shell back!"

"*She* has it!" the third goblin yelled, pointing at Rachel as she flew past him. "Let's grab her!"

"We can't reach her," the biggest goblin said with dismay, "There are too many of *these!*"

And he pointed down at the crowds of baby turtles at their feet. There were so many of them, they were creating a barrier between Rachel and the goblins. Rachel sighed with relief, clutching the shell piece more firmly.

The turtles were now slipping into the
water and swimming away as Pearl, Tess,
Rachel and Kirsty watched over them.
As the last ones scurried up to the water's
edge, the goblins glanced at each other.

"We can get the shell piece now!" the
biggest goblin shouted triumphantly.
"Come on!"

"We must get back to Fairyland right
away!" Tess cried, raising her wand.

There was a burst of golden sparkles and
Rachel and Kirsty saw Pearl shrink down
to fairy-size.

Then the four of them were whisked
away on a cloud of fairy magic, leaving
the goblins standing on the beach,
jumping up and down with rage.

A few seconds later, Tess, Rachel and
Kirsty were back at the Royal Aquarium.
Shannon, Ally, Amelie and Pia were
waiting for them, all looking very excited.
Pearl was already back in her tank of
water, next to Echo the dolphin, Silky the
seal and Scamp the penguin.

The other Magical Ocean Creatures
were thrilled to see Pearl back and they
splashed around in their tanks, calling out
a greeting.

"That was close!" Tess said with a smile.
"But we just made it!"

"Well done, all of you," Shannon
beamed at them. "Now let's replace
another missing piece of the Golden
Conch Shell!"

Rachel handed her the fragment of shell.

Shannon walked over to the table
where the pieces that had already been
found were sitting on a golden stand. As
Shannon held the shell piece out in front
of her, there was a flash of dazzling light
and the fragment sprang
from Shannon's hand
and fused magically
with the other
pieces, leaving no
visible crack or join.

   "Only three
more pieces to
find, and then our
Golden Conch Shell will be whole
once more!" Shannon said with delight.
She turned to Rachel and Kirsty. "It's
getting dark in Leamouth, so it's time to
send you home, girls. Thank you again."

"Thank you," the fairies chorused as a shower of magical sparkles from Shannon's wand floated down around Rachel and Kirsty. "See you again soon!"

The girls waved goodbye and, a few seconds later, found themselves back on the beach in Leamouth near their sandcastle.

"Wasn't that an exciting fairy adventure, Rachel?" Kirsty sighed happily. Then she gave a gasp. "Look at our sandcastle!"

A beautiful silver flag, glittering in the last rays of the sun, had been placed on top of one of the towers.

"Fairy magic!" Rachel said happily. "I'm so glad we found another shell piece, Kirsty. And we helped all the baby sea turtles get safely into the ocean, too."

"Yes, and now it's time for us to go
home!" Kirsty laughed, as they ran off
towards her gran's cottage. "The magic
did come to us in the end, didn't it,
Rachel? Even though it was a bit late
in the day!"

Rachel nodded. "I hope we find
another piece of the Magical Conch Shell
tomorrow," she added. "Four found, three
to go!"

RAINBOW
magic
The Ocean Fairies

Tess the Sea Turtle Fairy has found
her piece of the Golden Conch
Shell! Now Rachel and Kirsty
must help...

Stephanie the Starfish Fairy

Starry Skies

"The sea sounds so much louder at night, doesn't it?" Kirsty Tate said to her best friend Rachel Walker as they made their way down to Leamouth beach in darkness. The stars twinkled in the sky above them, and there was a full moon which cast silvery streaks on the tops of the waves.

"It feels completely different down here," Rachel agreed. "No noisy seagulls, no ice-cream van, no families making sandcastles…"

Kirsty smiled. "It's exciting," she said, hugging herself to keep warm as a cool breeze swept in from the sea. "Just like everything else about this holiday, really!"

Both girls were staying with Kirsty's gran for a week of the spring holidays, and Kirsty wasn't exaggerating when she said they'd been having an exciting time. The two friends had been helping the Ocean Fairies look for the seven missing pieces of a Magical Golden Conch Shell which had been smashed by mean Jack Frost. So far, they'd found four pieces of the shell and had four wonderful fairy adventures, but there were still three pieces left to find.

Tonight they'd been invited to join Gran's Astronomy Club for an evening picnic on the beach. The forecast was for a beautifully clear night, so Gran and her friends had brought down trestle tables

and picnic hampers to the beach, as well
as some impressive-looking telescopes.

Kirsty and Rachel helped set the food
out as the guests arrived and then, as the
sky grew darker still, Gran showed them
some of the constellations. "There are
eighty-eight constellations – or 'groups
of stars'," she told the girls, and pointed
upwards. "There's an easy one – the
Great Bear or, as we used to call it when
I was a girl, the Saucepan. Do you see the
shape of a saucepan up there?"

Rachel and Kirsty stared at where
she was pointing. "Yes!" Rachel cried
excitedly. "I see it. There's a handle, and
there's the pan."

"Oh yes!" Kirsty said, gazing up.

"Well, the 'saucepan' is part of the Great
Bear," Gran explained. "The handle is

the bear's tail, and the 'pan' is part of the bear's body. If you look carefully, you can see legs and a head shape, too." She smiled at the girls through the darkness. "It's a bit like joining up the dots to make a picture."

While Gran passed around cups of coffee from her thermos, Kirsty and Rachel continued to stare at the stars, trying to spot more pictures. "I can see a violin shape," Rachel said, showing Kirsty. "It's just like Victoria the Violin Fairy's."

"Oh yes," Kirsty said. "And there's a shoe shape, with ribbons attached, like Ruby the Red Fairy's shoe..."

The Ocean Fairies

Win Rainbow Magic goodies!

In every book in the Ocean Fairies series
(books 85-91) there is a hidden picture of a shell with a
letter in it. Find all seven letters and re-arrange them to
make a special Ocean Fairies word, then send it to us.
Each month we will put the entries into a draw and select
one winner to receive a Rainbow Magic sparkly T-shirt
and goody bag!

Send your entry on a postcard to Rainbow Magic Ocean
Fairies Competition, Orchard Books, 338 Euston Road,
London NW1 3BH. Australian readers should write to
Hachette Children's Books, Level 17/207 Kent Street,
Sydney, NSW 2000.
New Zealand readers should write to Rainbow Magic
Competition, 4 Whetu Place, Mairangi Bay, Auckland,
NZ. Don't forget to include your name and address.
Only one entry per child.
Final draw: 30th April 2011.

Have you checked out the

website at:

www.rainbowmagic.co.uk

Meet the Twilight Fairies

in September 2010!

Ava the Sunset Fairy
978-1-40830-906-3

Lexi the Firefly Fairy
978-1-40830-907-0

Zara the Starlight Fairy
978-1-40830-908-7

Morgan the Midnight Fairy
978-1-40830-909-4

Yasmin the Night Owl Fairy
978-1-40830-910-0

Maisie the Moonbeam Fairy
978-1-40830-911-7

Sabrina the Sweet Dreams Fairy
978-1-40830-912-4

Tess
the Sea Turtle
Fairy

Cut out this fairy and her
magical shapes then log on to
www.rainbowmagic.co.uk
to learn how to make
a magical mobile!

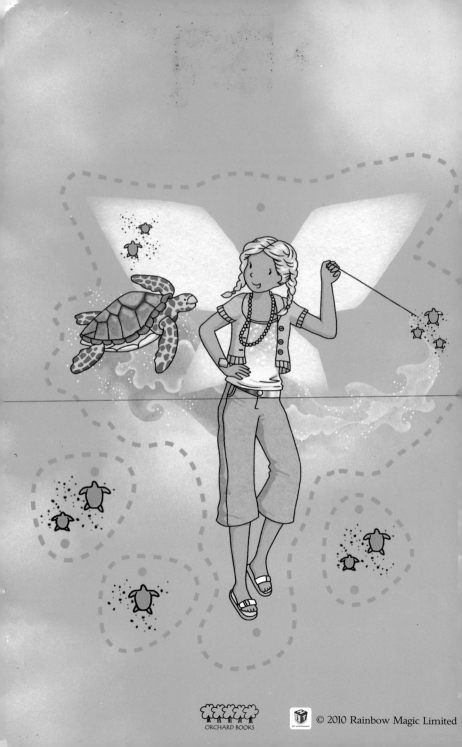